HUNTED

OUTRUN. OUTLAST. OUTWIT.

UK Legends

Edited By Allanah Jackson-James

First published in Great Britain in 2020 by:

Young Writers
Remus House
Coltsfoot Drive
Peterborough
PE2 9BF
Telephone: 01733 890066
Website: www.youngwriters.co.uk

Printed and bound in the UK by BookPrintingUK
Website: www.bookprintinguk.com
YB0439N

FOREWORD

IF YOU'VE BEEN SEARCHING FOR EPIC ADVENTURES, TALES OF SUSPENSE AND IMAGINATIVE WRITING THEN SEARCH NO MORE! YOUR HUNT IS AT AN END WITH THIS ANTHOLOGY OF MINI SAGAS.

We challenged secondary school students to craft a story in just 100 words. In this first installment of our SOS Sagas, their mission was to write on the theme of 'Hunted'. But they weren't restricted to just predator vs prey, oh no. They were encouraged to think beyond their first instincts and explore deeper into the theme.

The result is a variety of styles and genres and, as well as some classic cat and mouse games, inside these pages you'll find characters looking for meaning, people running from their darkest fears or maybe even death itself on the hunt.

Here at Young Writers it's our aim to inspire the next generation and instill in them a love for creative writing, and what better way than to see their work in print? The imagination and skill within these pages are proof that we might just be achieving that aim! Well done to each of these fantastic authors.

So if you're ready to find out if the hunter will become the hunted, read on!

CONTENTS

Olivia Clair Warrington (11)	64
Jenna Clay (13)	65
Aidan Daly (11)	66
Lucas Stephen Wenham (11)	67
Dylan Bowen-Knowles (12)	68
Mirena Dimitrova (12)	69
Jake Paul Quinn (11)	70
Liam Bowen (12)	71
Isabelle Livesley (12)	72
Grace Elder (11)	73
Henry Michael Laramee (11)	74

Shawlands Academy, Glasgow

Nikolas Thornton Miller (13)	75

St Columbanus' College, Bangor

Tyrell Kombo (14)	76
Grace Gunning	77
Katie Scott (13)	78
Seren Stewart (12)	79
Patryk Furman	80
Kenzie-Leigh Moore (11)	81
Bella McVey	82
Callum Price (13)	83
Jack O'Reilly (13)	84
Jaden Addis (11)	85
David Pim (13)	86
Rowan Montgomery (12)	87
Imogen Ward (13)	88
Matthew Bryans (13)	89
Abigail Morris (13)	90
Alisha McCausland (13)	91
Darragh Lynch (13)	92
Reece Erwin (12)	93
Lucy Bogle (12)	94
Lillie Griffiths (12)	95
Ross David McBride (14)	96
Grace Veale (13)	97
Taylor Quayle (12)	98
Jordan Kuruvilla (13)	99
Anastazia Bariova (12)	100
Amy Claney (13)	101

Olivia Maya Watson (12)	102
Cameron Wallace (13)	103
Remi-Rose Brotherston (13)	104
Dominik McCasland (13)	105
Nikola Kula (12)	106
Kiana McGimpsey (11)	107
Ruby Ward (13)	108
Jack Rendell (11)	109
Aaron Abraham (12)	110
Adrianna Andrijauskaite (13)	111
Bethany McClements (13)	112
Kavan McGrattan (12)	113
Charlie McInerney (12)	114
Oliver Elliott (12)	115
Stephanie Bell (13)	116
Reece Peck Bellorby	117

St Mary's CE High School, Cheshunt

Tayra Erturk (11)	118
Ariarne Charles-West (11)	119
Taylen Sanchez Salcedo (11)	120

St Ninian's High School, Kirkintilloch

Leah Kaye (11)	121

Welland Park Academy, Market Harborough

Cerys Heath (11)	122

THE STORIES

Kidnapped

Over five years ago, Lindsay was kidnapped by a serial killer. Fortunately for her, she escaped and was reunited with her dad and twin brothers, Luka and Liam. She was ecstatic about being home. However, the nightmares and night-terrors she got affected her every day. Her kidnapper had never been identified; the best description from Lindsay's knowledge was a thirty-seven-year-old man named Paul. Luka and Liam wanted him dead. However, Paul escaped to another town and thought he was safe... yet, the twins tracked him down, held a knife to his neck and said: "We want you dead."

Samantha Hayes (16)
Ashford College, Ashford

Those Glowing Yellow Eyes

I couldn't stop. If I did... I didn't know what would happen. However, whatever the thing was, it wouldn't stop either. Its pitch-black scales, glowing yellow eyes, almost a lizard but one which stood bipedal. Its teeth specially made for gripping, ripping and tearing anything in its way.

This thing chased me, it expeditiously followed me through the jungle. I still remember its roar, the sweating jungle felt abandoned. Nothing to be seen but a lot to be heard. I would never forget its glowing yellow eyes. They will always be in my dreams.

The glowing yellow eyes...

Sam Hawke
Ashford College, Ashford

The Chase Is On

It's my worst nightmare come to life. I'm being chased. I don't know where the others have gone. It was right behind them, right behind me. Camouflaged in a blanket of darkness, its trembling footsteps echoed throughout the abyss, engulfing the woodlands.

Its panting, its determined footsteps, all I feel now is my end coming closer. All I can do is run until I can't anymore, its footsteps getting closer, closer as if it's breathing down my chilling spine. I hear a stream up ahead, maybe a waterfall, my escape? I have one option, my only chance, my only escape.

Jack Turrell (18)
Ashford College, Ashford

Paranoia Tragedy

I stumbled down the gloomy street, feeling non-existent eyes staring intensely at me. My imagination was playing tricks on me, overthinking, as I imagine that I'm being hunted down like a sickened deer, trembling from the fear and paranoia of my mind. The wind breathed down the back of my neck like somebody was behind me, little did I know that someone was stalking me with fiery, devilish intent in their eyes.

Bang!

It all became quiet inside my mind as my large body hit the damp, moonlit floor with a thunderous clap. My body soon lying frozen and lifeless.

Adam Samuel Maxs Bonus Terry (17)
Ashford College, Ashford

The Accident

She's following me, down the wards of the hospital. She's watching me, through every room. I did nothing wrong, now she's hunting me down. She's hunting me till I'm dead. Like a deer in the woods, she's getting closer and closer. She will not stop until she catches me, I'm limping to my room, hiding in complete darkness. She's sharpening her knife outside, calling my name. She's done this before, I taught her... It was in an accident, I didn't mean to hurt her brother. She's coming, she's watching, she's hunting me for the last time... for good!

Lacey-Marie Hewer-Hewitt (16)
Ashford College, Ashford

The Mighty Sloth

The date was Friday the 13th of December. Everything was pitch-black. The sky, sun and sea were as black as coal. I couldn't see anywhere around me. The footsteps gradually got louder as it approached. Steadily, I walked onto the edge of the cliff. The sloth attached to my back yelped at the sight of the sudden drop. I quickly covered the sloth's mouth, stopping the scream. However, I heard the thing come rampaging towards me. All of a sudden, the sloth jumped off of my back and karate chopped the tree, killing the monster in one fell swoop.

Michael Towner (18)
Ashford College, Ashford

The Escape

The sirens wailed. I reached the eight-foot fence. I started to scramble up the barbed wire fence. I got halfway as my heart couldn't take much more of it. I looked down when I saw those massive fluffy balls with bold, googly eyes. I scrambled up the rest of the fence and I leapt over the mind-boggling fence.

I sprinted to the nearest, tallest tree where I climbed. The gates opened. I panicked, my heart stopped. I was tensing up. There was a loud, beaming voice that shouted, "You can't hide forever!"

The hunt was on.

Hollie Weeks (17)
Ashford College, Ashford

Hunted By The Stalker

I ran! Why wouldn't you when you're being hunted by the person that's stalking you?

It was about half-past eleven in the evening, the 26th of November 2016. I decided to go clubbing but when I saw him, I couldn't stay. I had to get out to survive. I was terrified but why wouldn't you be whilst running through dark alleyways on a foggy night in November, whilst there's always a chill in the air? Footsteps pounded behind me and voices shouted, "There she is!"

I was too late, sharp pain stopped me. I collapsed and everything went black.

Lauren Brocklehurst (17)
Ashford College, Ashford

Winners

They can't get to me here, right? It'd be hard at least; the fence surrounding the building loomed like a tower. The rain falling around me erased all thoughts. The thunder that followed rattled my entire body. *I've got to go inside but I'll be fine, I have to be.*

The building was eerily quiet but then I felt it. A long fingernail scratched my arm. *They're here and I'm now theirs.* I felt my eyes burn red-raw as my blood ran cold. Now to wait for the next 'soldier' and then convert them to the new winning team.

Bethany Cumber (16)

Ashford College, Ashford

YoungWriters
Est. 1991

The Climb

I walked through the field of dead crops crunching under my feet. I rustled through the waving grass, hoping to find shelter in this cloudy, open field. I shouted, "Hello!" in the hopes of finding people who hadn't lost their minds. An old couple approached me from seemingly nowhere. As they came closer, I saw the craziness in their eyes. The berzerk lady darted towards me with a knife with the old man in pursuit. I turned around and charged for the mountains, hoping to lose these savages. I grabbed onto the rocks but I fell, it was too late.

Pradesh Sunuwar (16)
Ashford College, Ashford

The Beast

Running, I always hated it. I always avoided it wherever possible but if I did that now, I'd certainly meet my death. She always told me we could only travel at night, I should have listened. Now, I sprinted as the beast relentlessly charged forward. I couldn't possibly outrun it, luckily they were as dumb as sheep. I darted left, then leapt forward and scaled the ladder. The beast copied the best it could, it darted left then crashed full force into the ladder. It stood at the bottom, it began to rage and lost my trail. I was safe.

Matthew Shaw
Ashford College, Ashford

Determination To Survive

In this world, it's doing what you can to survive. People will try to rob and kill ruthlessly so there are only two ways to survive: In a group, possibly with friends or own your own. Let me tell you this: I'm not gonna be taken out willingly or without it being on my own terms.

I heard a blood-curdling scream pierce through the silent day like a spear piercing a man's body. They were dead and whatever did it is heading this way. I unsheathed my machete, which was glinting in the sunlight. I was ready for the fight...

James Patrick Moran (19)
Ashford College, Ashford

Hunted

It was one shining night in New York, I was playing darts in a club. Suddenly, I felt a shiver down my spine like someone or something was hunting me down. I said to myself, "What was that?" It felt like a thousand spiders, crawling out of my ears.

It turned out to be my hunter, who lurks in a mysterious alley, trying to search out his target. The dark shadow hunter turned out to be a time-travelling robot, who can shape-shift into anything. It never stops until the target is terminated. It is greatly rewarded for it.

Hayden Moore (18)
Ashford College, Ashford

The Chocolate Heist

My heart thudded in my chest. He was after me. I could hear him around the corner. I crouched behind the tall trees, comprehending my choices. I never should have stolen that stupid chocolate bar.

He was getting closer, it was like I could feel his breath on my neck. In the distance, I saw a large pile of leaves that would be an ideal hiding spot. Should I run or stay? I didn't know. My breathing started to quicken as my heart raced more with every twig I heard break.

I felt a tap on my shoulder then... darkness.

Amy-Louise Lily Norrington (16)
Ashford College, Ashford

Hide-And-Seek

I couldn't breathe, I couldn't believe I couldn't find him. We started playing hide-and-seek but I couldn't see him. He hid first and I know I saw him go into the wardrobe but I looked in there many times and couldn't see him. I searched high and low, I emptied the wardrobe completely until there was nothing left but still couldn't find him anywhere. I started to panic and freak out. I had been hunting for him for about one to two hours by this point. I had lost track of time. I just wanted to find him!

Ebony Drew Terry (17)
Ashford College, Ashford

Hide From The KGB

The siren started. I wasn't safe. I saw many people run with panic in their eyes, I knew I had a few more minutes before I was targeted by the KGB. I had to find another location to hide in. However, I couldn't run for much longer, my ankle was caught by one of the traps. I started to lose blood fast, I only had thirty minutes before the KGB wiped out everything, so I decided to scream for help.
"Help, help!" I shouted but nobody was there until I heard my friend Harry's voice. I screamed his name.

Osemudiamen (Ose) Okpebholo (16)
Ashford College, Ashford

Mystery Forest

I raced into the shadowy, swampy, gloomy forest where I heard a thundering noise coming from inside. I took soft steps on the dead, dried-up crunchy leaves. The further I trembled in, the louder the dangerous noises got. It was like a monster - terrifying, horrifying. I looked from the corner of my worried eyes and I saw... I saw bright, mustard-yellow eyes, staring at me. I felt it go through my body like it was looking into my soul. I ran as fast as I could. A hand grabbed me by the waist and suddenly... darkness.

Kerry Jackson (17)
Ashford College, Ashford

Blood

Running. All I can do is run. I must rest and clear myself of the blood. My blood slowing at the absence of sound, I can't stop for long because Elijah and his pack will catch up to me. I'm safe for the moment, or so I thought. The exact moment my blood slows to normal, the ground opens up, consuming me. As I fall, my life and death flash before my eyes. Awaiting me at the bottom of the pit are large wooden spikes which pierce my heart, merging my blood with my victims. I laugh before silencing forever.

Malachy Bruno James Eastwood (16)
Ashford College, Ashford

Werewolves

I couldn't run for much longer, my legs started to hurt and I was becoming extremely tired. As I turned around they were still chasing me, the werewolves charging rapidly towards me like a pack of hounds waiting to be fed. Eventually, I reached the end and there was nowhere else to run, all I could do was climb the fence in front of me. I luckily managed to climb before the wolves caught up. The only problem was that the fence had barbed wire and was as sharp as knives, painfully digging into my bare hands.

Phoebe Eakers (16)
Ashford College, Ashford

Prison Break

The prison breakout area was packed like an airport on a hectic Christmas Eve. The sirens wailed, freedom was in sight. I was determined to not allow anything or anyone to stop me getting over the sky-high solid wall. My blood was pulsing through my veins as if I was turning into the Incredible Hulk. The seething anger within me propelled my hands and feet upon the wall and I started to climb as if I was Spider-Man chasing a villain but in this scenario, I was the villain being hunted down for my crime.

Rhys O'Sullivan (18)
Ashford College, Ashford

Shelter Hiding

It had to be here somewhere. The item was here a second ago; the others guarded our area as we could do nothing else. There were many alternatives but this was the most important one. I looked underneath our shelter, behind me, in the pockets of my coat, it wasn't there. The floor rumbled, I was being hunted. I jumped as high as I could to try and find this item and escape from the hunter that was not yet visible. The others stepped back and left me to deal with this. I panicked and my knees collapsed.

Hollie Richards (16)
Ashford College, Ashford

A Race For Survival

My heartbeat is slowing down but I can't catch my breath. They're close now, I can hear them. Their empty bodies, only filled with the desire of raw flesh. This city now lies empty and broken with a new source of life. Reincarnated. Slowly pulling myself up, a long, transparent needle pierces through my skin. An aching scream fills my head as I watch a dribble of warm red run down my arm. I feel a blind pair of eyes lock onto me. I feel the sudden urge to run as my adrenaline kicks in. Silence.

Imogen Bennett (17)
Ashford College, Ashford

The Countdown

I had twenty-four hours on the clock. Counting down, each second felt like I was being stabbed in the chest. From every tick to every tock, my mouth got drier and my chest got tighter. It was one life, one single life that wasn't worth living. I saved her, I promise, all I did was save her. I don't even wish I could go back, that poor little girl needed to die! She had no life, trapped in that house, being beaten every day.

I get trapped, no way out, with a clock that won't stop but counts down.

Chloe Daniels (17)
Ashford College, Ashford

Tsunami

My family and I were lying on a beach in a small village in the south of Spain. We could see in the distance a massive wave, soaring above the water and everyone on the beach sat up. Suddenly, the sirens wailed from the village hall and everyone on the beach darted as quick as they could to get to the highest point possible. When we reached the highest point at the top of a hill, we could see hundreds of terrified people being swept away in the ferocious tsunami. Only a small amount got up the hill.

Thomas Wood (16)
Ashford College, Ashford

They Thought Wrong

I knew I only had twenty-four hours left to escape before I was dead, I needed to move quickly. I was stuck inside an abandoned hospital with nothing but zombies and dead bodies. All I could smell was the flesh off of the deteriorating bodies, it was horrendous. I had to move as quietly as a mouse or otherwise, I wouldn't last a minute with all of the zombies coming through the main door. So I had to try and find a fire exit and get out. Every step I took I was crunching on bundles of bones.

Lewis Patterson (17)
Ashford College, Ashford

Run For Your Life

I can't run for much longer, my legs felt so weak, like mush. I look back every few seconds to see if I'm still being pursued but every time I look, they get closer and closer. Instead of running, I decide to hide. So, I hastily creep over to a nearby tree and hide there till their footsteps fade into silence. I look around, thinking it is over until I feel a hand touch my shoulder. I jolt and land on the floor. I look up and notice they want to help me. I then realise I am safe.

Amber Fishlock
Ashford College, Ashford

The Rabid Frog

I have been kidnapped. I wake up in a foul-smelling place. I look around and see specific signs that give me what I need to know. I must find four numbers to a vault but there is a frog on the loose. I am now stuck in a maze with a rabid frog. If it licks me, I will become paralysed and eaten. I find the numbers and the vault but no sign of the frog. I become scared and petrified about this thing. I have now opened the vault and when I did, I accidentally unleashed hell.

Rashane Cooray (16)
Ashford College, Ashford

A Hunter's Apocalypse

As I silently gazed down the sight of my parker hale M81, I calmly searched for stray walkers. I was hit with a strong sense of nostalgia from before the collapse. Every summer I would take a trip out with my young lad, we would sit in what we used to call the 'deer seeker,' a camouflaged cabin that we'd sit and hunt deer in... What I'd give to have him back.
Bang! Killing walkers was never quite the same as deer, it really didn't have the same feeling.

Max Coppin (18)
Ashford College, Ashford

Wolf Hunt

It's not safe now they know, I must get out of here. I packed my clothes as fast as I could. I was packing like I was under a time limit. All of a sudden, I rapidly turned around and sprinted out of the cramped hut I was staying in. I turned around quickly and saw that I was being hunted by a pack of wolves that were looking like they wanted to kill me. They were running like bullets. I tried to sprint as fast as I could but my legs were killing me.

Courtney Black (17)
Ashford College, Ashford

Werewolves

I was abandoned in my car with no one around me. In the corner of my mirror, I saw a pack of werewolves coming from behind my car with their yellow fangs pointing out. They got closer and closer to my car. As they got closer, I started to get more anxious. I started to think that this was the last day of my life. When they were next to my window, I all of a sudden heard a gunshot and I looked in my mirrors. There was a man there, he saved my life from them.

Molly Cooper (17)
Ashford College, Ashford

Running To The Motor

The lights were flashing blue and red on the road behind the boy and I. The light pierced the night sky like flares. We were dashing and weaving between people shopping and walking. We were heading to the motor, I didn't care about the air force ones I was wearing. We were bumping and crashing into people. We all had around one million pounds on us. The motor was behind the Ritz. As we got to the motor, we all jumped in and got away in perfect timing.

Tim Sheppard (16)
Ashford College, Ashford

The Boy And The Bear

The hunt begins... the young, terrified boy scopes out his best option. His scared eyes focus on a dark, dense forest. His tense, tender heart is racing at one hundred miles per hour as he flies through the dense carpet of orange leaves. The ten-foot dark brown bear crawls aggressively, almost breaking into a canter. The frail boy's legs start to weaken as he gets deeper into the land of darkness. His small shoes lose traction on the green moss...

Lewis Agius (16)
Ashford College, Ashford

Temple Hunt

I still have nightmares about it. We were running through a never-ending forest, it was so dark. I couldn't remember what happened, I just woke up running and I only knew one thing, I had to keep running because whatever was chasing me was going to keep chasing me. If it got me that would be it, game over. After a while, the scenery started to change to a temple kind of place with a bridge. I turned just for a split second and saw the beast...

Thomas Roberts
Ashford College, Ashford

Sneaking Silently

I listen carefully and I hear the delicate tapping of a large pack of wolves, searching for their next meal. I try to stay silent, to avoid any sort of confrontation with the pack. I sneak out of my camp and head towards the next part of the mountain but as I walk, I am seen and the chase is on! I run as fast as I can but the pack is right behind me, right on my tail! I see a large gap in the rocks ahead. I think I might be able to jump...

Nathan Heseldine (17)
Ashford College, Ashford

The Hustle

It's not safe now they know... our future is on that lorry. I'm sweating, they want what we have! We are running through the dark streets and they are following us. We flash through each alley but they still keep up. We crash... it's over for us! We step out of the car into the smoke.

Bang! Bang! They shoot at me. I run and jump off the bridge onto the ferry with the lorry! I am safe but my friend is not...

Aimee Kilsby (16)
Ashford College, Ashford

The Bird Cage

Hope for my freedom withers away, like that of a lifeless bird trapped in a wire cage with no room to stretch my dull, aching wings. However, like any trapped bird, I will find a way to escape, to fly to my freedom. I'll need to calculate this correctly, I'll need to be as agile and as quick as a vulture on fresh prey. Desperate to prove my innocence, I plan my escape. After all, a bird always finds a way to escape its cage.

Caitlin Andrews (19)
Ashford College, Ashford

The Hunt

Panicked and scared, I sat behind the dumpster beneath the undercarriage. I was as white as a canvas, startled by the object which I had just seen. I remember every detail from head to toe as if it was in front of me. I cannot bear to think about what it could've done to me if I hadn't run. Its fearsome posture and threatening appearance startled me to the point of panic, nothing could stop his vicious rage.

Charlie Fewins-Orchard
Ashford College, Ashford

The Deserted Shack

I couldn't run for much longer, the ferocious wolves were chasing me and my car broke down. There was nowhere to run or hide until I came across an abandoned shack in a snowy, deserted forest. As I approached the shack, I could hear the wolves getting closer and closer every second. Luckily the shack door blew open and as soon as I ran in, I shut the door and locked it but I knew it wouldn't hold for long.

Dylan Van Graan (16)
Ashford College, Ashford

Through The Twisted Trees

I bolted as expeditiously as an Olympic one hundred metre sprinter through the twisted trees. Every five seconds I looked over my shoulder to see if he was still behind me. I couldn't see a thing, it was as dark as a raven. Suddenly, I slammed hard to the ground as I hit something large and heavy. I looked above me and stood there was my killer.

Amelia Skivington-Wright (16)
Ashford College, Ashford

In The Graveyard

I couldn't run for much longer as my livid stepmother was running after me. Although, we hadn't realised we were alone in a pitch-black graveyard. We heard a loud bellow from behind a wall. We hesitated, unaware of what was behind it. I walked towards the wall, noticing a mysterious figure stood in the shadows. Shivers travelled down my spine as the moonlight highlighted an eerie outline. As the shadows bellowed once more, my heart raced double the pace. I looked around for my stepmother but she had gone. I was alone...
What could this frightening something be?

Abigail Levy
Hope Academy, Newton-Le-Willows

The Ones That Got Away

The people entered the house. They had just come from the neighbour's yard. He was watching them.

Meanwhile, the police were on the phone giving advice. They were fully occupied so they had no troops to send.

They were making their way up the stairs to his room, he could hear them chanting unhuman songs. He could feel his heart starting to pound rapidly, the officer on the phone told him to stay calm but he couldn't. He told the officer to be quiet as they were outside of his bedroom.

"They're not human!" he panted. *Bang!* They got him.

Adam Bowen (12)
Hope Academy, Newton-Le-Willows

Run, Run, Run

I couldn't run for much longer... or even at all. They were getting closer, a lot closer. We didn't exactly know what we were running from but we carried on. We could hear the monster's footsteps banging on the road behind us. *Bang! Bang! Bang!* They were really close now! We couldn't escape. Not now. They were saying something to us, we couldn't hear them though. Where were we? I was shaking, full of fright, we thought they might be humans but we didn't have enough time to think about that. We were just running, running into the midnight sky...

Eleanor Williams (12)
Hope Academy, Newton-Le-Willows

The Jump

Felix was ready in the balloon. His team was ready for him to go to the edge of space.
He could feel himself going faster and faster. At the precise time he was told, Felix pulled the cord for the parachute. Nothing. He tried it again. Nothing. His stomach started churning. He didn't feel safe anymore. His team started worrying.
He pulled it one last time and it deployed. His team all cheered as Felix stumbled to his feet. This mission was very successful and all the people who watched (8 million) were very proud of this almost impossible task.

Seren James (11)
Hope Academy, Newton-Le-Willows

The Freefall

Panic, stress, determination, nerves were running through his body. A tight-packed space surrounded him as he was slowly drifting up.

"Okay, we're there. Prepare for countdown," Felix heard out of his speaker. With his palms sweating and his hands shaking under his suit, "Yes, ready for freefall," he stuttered anxiously. He had never been so worried. As he took one final breath, he jumped down into the atmosphere. He went as quick as a snap of a finger. Then, breaking eight world records and the sound barrier, he had done it.

Patrick Chandler Kelly (12)
Hope Academy, Newton-Le-Willows

D-Day

It was D-Day and I was on a boat with about thirty-six other soldiers, crammed in a boat. We were all very scared but still determined to fight for our country. We heard the captain shout, "Thirty seconds!" and had our guns ready at hand. The door opened and what I saw was scary. The soldiers in front of me had bullet wounds with blood spraying, people leaping from the boat and drowning. The worst part was the beach. *Boom! Boom!* Limbs flew everywhere, my friends were dead. I was the lucky one, I was the only man left standing.

Quinn Moran (12)
Hope Academy, Newton-Le-Willows

The Freefall

Leaning out of the capsule, I could see a great blue ball of land and sea. From space, I couldn't quite make out the details, it all became a blur of blue and green. Adrenaline rushed through my body. I slowly fell into space. Before I knew it I was tumbling uncontrollably at an immense speed! Fog began to cloud my visor. I couldn't see. My heart was racing, panic struck. I reached back to release the parachute. The fog cleared. Suddenly, the shape of the land came into view. Earth's gravity pulled me towards the ground with a thud.

Melissa Rose Wilkinson (12)
Hope Academy, Newton-Le-Willows

Felix's Freefall

The brave Felix had been waiting for this all his life, to fall from the edge of space! To break the sound barrier! Falling at a rapid speed of 833.9mph, Felix was petrified. Would he live? Would he make it? Shivers shot up and down his spine as he violently span towards Earth. All he could think about was landing safely. As he swiftly plummeted down to land, the screaming and cheering got louder and louder.

10 metres left... 9... 8... The people were becoming clear. He was close. His feet could now touch the ground... *Thud!*

Keira Marshall (12)
Hope Academy, Newton-Le-Willows

The Freefall

I looked out the pod to see... the Earth! It was amazing, beautiful and I couldn't believe I was gonna jump twenty-five miles! The pod door opened and a wave of nausea suddenly hit me, but I couldn't stop. I jumped. The pressure. I was going down headfirst and terrifying thoughts filled my head. *What if my parachute doesn't open? What if I don't land safely?* I blocked the thoughts in my head and pulled the chute. As my eyes opened I couldn't believe it... I landed! It was the most thrilling day of my life!

Madeleine Holligan (11)
Hope Academy, Newton-Le-Willows

The Freefall

Felix is a crazy man and he tried to beat a world record. His team, Red Bull, were supporting him through his jump but something went wrong, something dreadful...

Felix was preparing for this moment for years. He wanted to beat this world record.

Today he was going to jump out of the pod. He was scared for multiple reasons. He tried not to worry about it but he couldn't help it. As he pulled his cord it didn't work and his team were worrying! But in the end, he landed safely but it gave him nightmares for years!

Charlie Whittle (12)
Hope Academy, Newton-Le-Willows

The Snowy Figure

I woke up in a deep sweat. I looked outside, the snow was crisp and untouched, the air was cold and sharp. Putting my head back on the pillow, I saw something, someone in the corner of my eye. I thought to myself, *who would be walking in that weather so early in the morning?* I looked again at the figure, gone. Something was clearly wrong. I heard a *bang!* Then footsteps. Whatever it was, it was coming up the stairs. My wooden door creaked open. The suspense was killing me, I turned on the light... nothing!

Lily May Hughes (12)
Hope Academy, Newton-Le-Willows

Freefall Jump

I was close to twenty miles up, only another four to go. Sweat dripped down my forehead, my hands were trembling. I was petrified. The pod signalled its noise to jump. The door opened. My seatbelt was undone and I stood up. For five minutes I stood, thinking *what if this goes wrong?*
But after a while, I jumped. Spinning and turning, I felt sick. After a while of falling, I knew my parachute should have opened by now. So I worried. Two miles from Earth and I was still falling, I knew I wouldn't make it...

Harrison Schofield (12)
Hope Academy, Newton-Le-Willows

Prison Break

The alarms are wailing, I know they are here. I hear footsteps getting louder, they are here. I hear voices getting louder, they must be close. I have an explosive device in my front pocket but the question is, where do I throw it? I see shadows reflecting on the walls as the light of the guard tower shines on the figures. I can tell they are close, goosebumps are starting to appear on my skinny arms as I haven't eaten in days. There are two ways out, either the sewer or under the barbed wire fence. What happens now?

Charlie Gerrity (12)
Hope Academy, Newton-Le-Willows

Freefalling

My skin felt clammy. I fell into a freefall, spinning and tumbling down and down. Would I ever stop? My mind started to run wild, the thought of death was inevitable. Then all of a sudden calm washed over me as I stopped spinning and falling and came to a soft landing. My ordeal was over. Relief rushed through my body. I would be able to see my family again and this wasn't the last chapter of my life. Afterwards, the sense of accomplishment made me feel proud. I went home a national treasure. Don't take life for granted.

April Baker (11)
Hope Academy, Newton-Le-Willows

The Freefall

I was twenty-five miles above the ground. I couldn't believe that I was about to jump. But I wanted to enter the world records for my family. Then I did it. I jumped! As I was plummeting towards the ground thoughts raced through my head: *Was I going to survive? Was my parachute going to open? How were my family going to react?* Then I realised I was nearing the ground. Suddenly I pulled my parachute cord and it opened! For a split second I thought I would never see the light of day again. But I survived!

Evie Fenerty (11)
Hope Academy, Newton-Le-Willows

The Freefall

As I jumped my heart began to slam against my chest. I could only think about all the bad things that could happen. It was going well until just as I suspected, my parachute wasn't coming out. I yelled in fear of dying. I could see myself hitting the floor full force. I was scared, knowing eventually I would die. I began to cry. I was shouting for my life. I knew deep down nobody would come. A sharp rock plunged through me.

I woke up and realised it was all just a dream and I was fine, nothing happened.

Amelia Grace McNicholas (11)
Hope Academy, Newton-Le-Willows

The Tsunami Of Nightmares

I still have nightmares about it. I remember it so vividly as if it were a dream. We were close to losing our lives. Everything happened so fast, I didn't know what was happening to me. So many souls were affected that day by the water. No one was expecting it to happen. I remember that first wave hitting the land as if the world was just crumbling into tiny pieces. The look on people's faces was terrifying. No one knew what was happening. We had to get out. I had no idea that this would affect my entire life.

Alana Underhill (13)
Hope Academy, Newton-Le-Willows

Felix And His Epic Adventure

When Felix was a young boy he decided he wanted to do something dangerous when he grew up. In fact, he wanted to go up into space but in a balloon and jump out of it, and this is what he did.

When he was thirty he went up into space and jumped out of the balloon. Only when he did that he started running out of oxygen. Luckily, he just had enough oxygen to land safely, only his parachute wouldn't open so he pressed and pressed. Just before he landed the parachute opened and he landed nice and safely.

Millie Anslow (11)

Hope Academy, Newton-Le-Willows

Criminals Escape Prison

Three new criminals were captured and brought into the local prison.
It was the next day and they said: "We need to get out of this place, we have only been given stale bread and warm water."
They decided to make an escape plan. It was two weeks later and they had made a plan but they needed to get some spoons from the lunch hall so they could dig through the walls. Five months later the hole they had made was finally big enough for the big escape. The police put out an investigation for them.

Nathan Swift (12)
Hope Academy, Newton-Le-Willows

The Jump

Felix was always a brave kid. He loved doing challenging things like running marathons. But that was nothing compared to what he wanted to do. Felix had one thing wrong with what he wanted to do - he was actually scared of it. He wanted to skydive. So he practised day in day out and eventually he was ready. He was ready to do the one thing he had been scared of his whole entire life.
When the balloon was pumped up he flew up all the way to the edge of space and he did it. Yes, he jumped out!

Tyler Hunter (12)
Hope Academy, Newton-Le-Willows

Death Awaits

I woke up, had breakfast and dressed up. Suddenly, there was a knock on the door. I slowly walked to the door, looked through the peephole and saw a white, tall, pale man. I slowly opened the door but saw no one. I thought I was crazy until I looked down, a big box with my name written in red, bold text was there. I took it inside and opened it up. Inside there was only one thing. A syringe with a green liquid inside of it. Suddenly, a siren went off. The dead woke up from their eternal slumber.

Roberto Gabriel Ungureanu (13)
Hope Academy, Newton-Le-Willows

24 Hours Of Nightmares

Bang! Bang! The gunshots still ring in my ears, it feels like it was yesterday when that figure jumped out of nowhere and shot Ben! I had to run or I would be dead too, so I sprinted as fast as I could and eventually I had lost him. Well, that's what I thought. I hid behind this huge brick wall and called the police, they said they would be there in no time but minutes turned into hours and when I could hear the sirens, I thought it was all over. But out of nowhere, he was there!

Cole Howlett
Hope Academy, Newton-Le-Willows

The Greatest Fall Of Mankind

There I was, twenty-five miles above Earth. There was only one way down - to jump. What if the parachute didn't open? I had to jump or else I'd be stuck in space forever! I looked down. I had to jump. Now.

I lifted one leg up and jumped! I felt nothing as I fell, only my ears going numb. I got hold of my cord, this could kill me if this didn't work. I pulled it... To my luck, my parachute opened! The rest of the way I glided down until my feet were safely on the floor. Finally! Home!

Chloe Doran (11)
Hope Academy, Newton-Le-Willows

The Plunge

I jumped, falling down to Earth at a supersonic pace. The view of the globe was mindblowing. Then I started to become unstable. Suddenly, I started to rotate at a faster pace, then faster then faster. The world was spinning before my eyes, as if I'd done 1,000 front flips. I began to fall unconscious. I started to lose sight and hearing. Suddenly, I saw that I was terribly close to the ground, but I heard something in my ear. It was the director telling me to pull a cord. So I did.

Leo Cunnington (11)
Hope Academy, Newton-Le-Willows

The Freefall

Frozen, I got shot up to space. I still couldn't believe that I was really doing this. Imagine if I didn't make it. As I finally got where I needed to be, space, my teammates were telling me that it could go wrong and that made me crack in my own skin.

Suddenly I jumped out of the pod... I blacked out... My team were telling me to wake up and quickly get my parachute out. Which I did. I could see my team cheering for me while recording as I slowly came down from the sky.

Olivia Clair Warrington (11)
Hope Academy, Newton-Le-Willows

On The Run

I couldn't run for much longer. I'd been running for days. No food. No drink. I knew I was going to get caught sooner or later. It was now or never. I was on the run for shooting someone in the head in the middle of the day.
I really needed a drink, I was walking until I heard sirens wailing. I walked to a shop but I didn't have any money, so I drank from a lake. The sirens were closer, I turned around and he was there. Sherrif Donald. He put me in handcuffs and into the car.

Jenna Clay (13)
Hope Academy, Newton-Le-Willows

The Freefall

I was in the pod waiting to take off. Me and my team and my family and friends' hearts were beating faster than lightning. Everybody knew if this went to plan it would be the greatest ever freefall jump.

I finally took off in my pod carried by a hot-air balloon. When I made it to the top, I opened the door and took a look down and it was then when I wanted to turn back. But I knew there was none of that now so I just jumped and it felt like hours. I pulled my parachute!

Aidan Daly (11)
Hope Academy, Newton-Le-Willows

The Tower Of Gloom And Doom

"Let's go on a hunt," they said... "It'll be fun," they said... Well, here we are in the tower of doom. It is haunted, it is dark but I have to get out, most of the clues lead us to a dead end! One clue left, we're close. The sirens wail, we follow the lights and noises. The clue is in the wailing sirens, 999 is the answer to unlock the door. I can't run any longer but I do, we make it out safe. Maybe the next hunter will be caught...

Lucas Stephen Wenham (11)

Hope Academy, Newton-Le-Willows

Hunt For The World Record

Felix was more than a mile away from the stratosphere but something had gone wrong, his visor was fogged. He had to skydive blind. Another problem had occurred, the balloon had popped. Felix was rocketing down to Earth at such speed. Quickly, he opened the capsule and fell out. He was falling at such speed he broke the sound barrier. Felix had to open his parachute but it wasn't working. What was he going to do? Just fall there and die? He had to do something, but what?

Dylan Bowen-Knowles (12)
Hope Academy, Newton-Le-Willows

Hide-And-Seek

I had twenty-four hours: I'd turn into minced meat if it found me during that time. I knew I would have to keep my eyes out for it. Why was I here in the first place? Why was I dragged here? My surroundings were dark, I was dizzy and really weak. I managed to find a wide crevice in one of the rocks around me; I crawled inside. I felt like I was being watched... because I was. There it stood, the creature glaring at me. Its eyes were fixed only on me. I knew I was dead.

Mirena Dimitrova (12)
Hope Academy, Newton-Le-Willows

Felix's Freefall

As he was going up in his pod, he looked down at the Earth, the emotions going through his body. He could die. He pressed the button to open the door. He was ready, but not at the same time. But no matter what, he went for it. He dived down. He was thinking about whether he was going to make it down. As he could see the ground clearer he pulled the cord and his parachute shot out and he slowly descended to the ground. His team welcomed him back to Earth.

Jake Paul Quinn (11)
Hope Academy, Newton-Le-Willows

The Freefall

It was time to go! Felix was ready. The balloon was floating into the air. It was held down by a crane. They were ready. Felix went off and floated up into the air. Seconds felt like minutes, minutes felt like hours. It finally became time to jump. Hesitantly he jumped. Falling through the sky rapidly, he fell and fell and fell until it was time to pull the chute. He pulled it. It sprang out and the team was thrilled that he made it back alive.

Liam Bowen (12)
Hope Academy, Newton-Le-Willows

The Jump

The rocket lifted. It began the journey to space. I watched the crowd cheer and chant. I had only a few minutes before I would be twenty-five miles in space.

I made it. I looked around at the 360° view of Earth but then it dawned on me that now was the time to jump. I began to prepare frantically for the jump. As fast as light I began to plummet towards the Earth's atmosphere. As fast as it had begun I was back on the ground. Safe at last.

Isabelle Livesley (12)
Hope Academy, Newton-Le-Willows

The Freefall

Felix started his journey to break the world record fall. He planned to and he did. He went up in a small pod carried up in a hot-air balloon without the basket. When he was twenty-four miles up in the air the pod door opened and he jumped. It took him four minutes to get back to Earth. He successfully got back to Earth!

Grace Elder (11)
Hope Academy, Newton-Le-Willows

The Freefall

There he was, twenty-five miles into the air. There was no going back now. Seconds away from jumping, he wondered if it was possible to make it. Unexpectedly, he leapt and in seconds he was gone. He tumbled and flew, this led to him losing balance. He still had a few miles to go when he safely opened his parachute.

Henry Michael Laramee (11)
Hope Academy, Newton-Le-Willows

Breathless

I pulled up by a tree. Breathless and light-headed, I knew I couldn't stop but I had to. It was lurking in the shadows. I could feel its presence and it could feel mine. I had to pick my moment to run. The gap was closing, it was now or never. Run!
I ran as fast as I could. No turning back. I kept running but I knew I'd have to stop at some point. I pulled up by another tree. Total silence reassured me. I felt safe. But then something felt wrong. I felt pain. I felt nothing. I exhaled.

Nikolas Thornton Miller (13)
Shawlands Academy, Glasgow

The Organ Harvester

Our neighbourhood was as quiet as ditched ruins. No one dared to leave their houses. There was a rumour circulating about the 'Organ Harvester'. Every morning, an elderly citizen would be declared dead.

One night, my friend and I took the brave decision to take down this mystery. What we saw was just enough to blind a human being. We saw him carrying a mattock stained in blood which linked with all the postmortems. Surprisingly, we saw human organs in his vintage cooler box. From that moment, we ran faster than shadows. Every inhalation felt like needles stabbing my throat.

Tyrell Kombo (14)
St Columbanus' College, Bangor

Ski Slaughter

We were having so much fun on our ski holiday. We were standing in front of the chair lift with our skis on. It scooped us up. From the moment we got on, we knew it didn't feel right. It started speeding up. It got faster. It started going backwards, faster than anything I've ever seen. We couldn't see anything but blurriness. We were all terrified and people started jumping off. They were breaking limbs, others were being thrown. There were piles of people. My mind was blank. I couldn't think. I survived. Many didn't.
I still have nightmares.

Grace Gunning
St Columbanus' College, Bangor

Frozen In Time

The sirens wailed, my heart was racing. I heard some branches snap. *Bang! Bang!* On the side of the shed. Laughing, they started laughing. I got very scared. *Snap!* Branches snapped as they walked towards the door. The door flew open and I fell through the floor. I opened my eyes, I looked around and saw swings and playsets. I saw little kids, frozen in time, everyone and everything had stopped. I saw some random man running at me with a gun, ready to shoot. He said, "Three, two, one..."
I closed my eyes for the last time.

Katie Scott (13)
St Columbanus' College, Bangor

Running

The sirens wailed, I was sore all over. Blood, a pool of blood. *Who was bleeding?* I wondered. I went to get up. I couldn't. I found blood on my shirt. "I am bleeding!" I looked in front of me. A bullet. Covered in blood. "Where am I?" Then it all came back to me. I was running, running for my life, away from them. The keepers. They must've called the police! *I need to get out of here! They'll be onto me any minute! Where will I go?*
"Stay where you are! You have been hunted," came a voice.

Seren Stewart (12)
St Columbanus' College, Bangor

Wanted

He couldn't run for much longer, he was the person wanted for killing several innocent people. He escaped from prison. It reached midnight, I went to sleep. I couldn't sleep because I had lots of nightmares about it. The next day reached, I heard my phone ringing. A deep voice said, "I will kill your family."
I went downstairs and locked all of my doors up, then I went to call my dad but he wouldn't answer. I heard loud banging at the door. He smashed the door. My brother grabbed a gun and shot him, he died.

Patryk Furman
St Columbanus' College, Bangor

Deadly Hide-And-Seek

One day, a girl went to the forest with her mum, dad and big brother. She wanted to play hide-and-seek and they did, the girl and the brother were hiding, the parents were seeking. They heard a scream and they ran, they couldn't find them or where the scream came from. But then they heard a man saying, "Shut up, they might hear you and then I'll get arrested."
Then, they heard a final scream and they ran to the scream and they saw their daughter's dead body.
(PS I was the killer, I'll come for you next!)

Kenzie-Leigh Moore (11)
St Columbanus' College, Bangor

Hunted

I was scared. I ran into the lift and I got out at the top floor.
There he was, standing there with a gun in his hand. He
started shooting. I started to run. I thought I had escaped.
Five minutes later, he appeared again. I went and hid and
called the police, "I am being hunted."
"What do you mean by 'being hunted'?" the police said.
"There is someone coming for me with a gun in his hand!"
"Okay, we are on our way," the police came and saved me
and put the man in jail.

Bella McVey
St Columbanus' College, Bangor

Criminal Mastermind

The sirens wailed... there had been a casualty in room 816. Agent 1863 left in an escape pod. Little did they know, I sent that escape pod... I was 1863.

Now I am known as 1984. I must leave, now. I ask if I can be tasked with hunting them down. The hunter becomes the hunted. Upon landing, my watch bleeps. I have been found out. Commander Shaun says, "You! You're agent 1863." Ironically, I laugh maniacally, "Hahaha," and smash my watch. Before they arrive, I gather tools and then I see a camp. After paying them, I hide.

Callum Price (13)
St Columbanus' College, Bangor

The Hunt Is On

Bang! Gunshots were fired, bodies flew through the air, the prison was chaos. Prisoners were left, right and centre. Prison guards tackled prisoners and handcuffed them. I was running for my life. I found a car, I hid in it for as long as I could. I heard police cars driving past. Luckily, no one saw me, or that's what I thought. The car door opened, two people got in the car but they looked like homeless people the way they were dressed. Thinking of that distracted me, they looked back and found me. We screamed.

Jack O'Reilly (13)
St Columbanus' College, Bangor

Hunted Me!

Where can I hide? Where can I go?
From England all the way to South America, two years of running. They might finally catch me. I was accused of ten murders in 2020, they haven't given up on trying to find me. I can't sleep because of the sound of sirens, helicopters and dogs.

Once, they found out where I was, I had to run as fast as I could, they haven't seen me since. I really don't want to live my life like this but I can't give myself in, I'll die in prison. Please, please, help me.

Jaden Addis (11)
St Columbanus' College, Bangor

Test Subject War

I had twenty-four hours to give myself up or I would be shot on sight. I hid in a bush, all I could hear was a lot of cars and voices saying: "Test subject 132670-27, you have twelve hours left. Come out now if you don't want to be killed." They were all unknown voices but they all were guards for sure.

I had got myself into a safe zone, that means they couldn't get me. That's what I thought. They somehow got in the safe zone I was in and had eyes on me.

Bang! "Help!"

David Pim (13)

St Columbanus' College, Bangor

Lost Brother

I can't run for much longer. My throat is dry, my torso aches. My tummy roars as I pull myself through the damp woods. The man that took my brother will pay. With his life. Scared that something might jump out, I make it back to my cabin. I grab an axe and my dad's pistol. I try to load the pistol and end up shooting the shed window! Thank goodness I escaped but it's not about me! It's me, getting my brother alive. Dragging myself up the woods to the man's house, I feel sick. He will be scary!

Rowan Montgomery (12)
St Columbanus' College, Bangor

The Girl Next Door

It was the day of the year for children to dress up but not for Leah, Leah was petrified of Halloween. If she heard a knock on the door, she would freeze like an ice cube until she couldn't hear anymore crying from outside. She heard a witch laughing, as she walked down the driveway it got louder. Her knees felt like arrows were stabbing her. Her hands were sweating until she saw a white figure reaching his hand out saying, "Welcome to your new home, the land of the dead!" She closed her eyes but it wasn't a dream.

Imogen Ward (13)
St Columbanus' College, Bangor

Hot Pursuit

I was chasing them. I was close. I could hear their footsteps getting louder, I thought that if I ran a bit quicker, I might catch them. After chasing them for a while, I heard a noise which I couldn't make out. I then caught sight of the prisoners that had escaped. They were crossing the train tracks. I heard the train when it passed, the prisoners had disappeared. I looked around for a bit but the prisoners had escaped. The police sent a search patrol for them for a few days afterwards but they were gone.

Matthew Bryans (13)
St Columbanus' College, Bangor

What I Saw Through The Window

Bang! Why did I have to see this?

It was a bright, beautiful sunny Saturday morning. My friends and I decided to go shopping before it all happened... We were skipping like gazelles down the road when we passed the jewellers with diamonds shining as bright as the stars. Suddenly, it felt like it was in slow motion! I saw a stranger holding a gun to the shopkeeper's head! I froze outside the window, my feet were stuck to the ground like glue. In a flashing moment, the man shot him in the head.

Abigail Morris (13)
St Columbanus' College, Bangor

The Run

The sirens wailed, my heart thumped, we were close after years of being on the run because of being hunted. I started to sweat, the car pulled up right beside our police car but it wasn't just one or two people that left, it was five... My heart dropped, my face went paler, my legs went like jelly. The worst nightmare of my life became even more real than ever. I was escorted by the man and woman from the front of the car but they weren't who I thought they were, they were one of them. It went black...

Alisha McCausland (13)
St Columbanus' College, Bangor

Bank Robbery

The sirens wailed. We were running through the bank, ready to bust through the door carrying heavy bags of money that were weighing us down. We knew we had a long journey ahead to get to the escape car where we arranged to meet them. We bust through the door and turned right up the alleyway. We ascended up the hill. We had practised this routine for weeks in advance, we were moving at a good pace but we could hear the sirens gaining on us. This was the hard part, we had to cross the road without being spotted.

Darragh Lynch (13)
St Columbanus' College, Bangor

Slender-Hulk

I've been running for hours, away from this man or 'thing'. I don't know what it is. Something like the Hulk and Slender put together.

Crunch! Oh, my goodness. He is close. What should I do? Oh, no! I see his white mask and his tall legs and very long arms. What should I do? I know, I'll run in the other direction and hope I lose him. One hour later, I hope he doesn't find me up here in this massive tree.

"Where are you?" he says. I don't make a sound.

Reece Erwin (12)
St Columbanus' College, Bangor

The Figure

I hear them... I have no choice. I dive into the monstrous river below and land with unbearable pain in my leg. The gusts of wind whisk me away into the rapids, the current so powerful I can't swim away. I crash into rocks, my leg now hanging by the little flesh attached. I'm so cold that I am oblivious to my surroundings. I glance over the river and see that it twists into... a waterfall. I desperately grasp a rock, my body lying halfway over my death and then a figure approaches.
"You betrayed me."

Lucy Bogle (12)
St Columbanus' College, Bangor

Run For It

I couldn't run for much longer. They were coming for me. The next morning I woke somewhere I'd never seen before, it looked like I was in a boarding school. I got my shoes on and went to open the door when I felt a hard tap on my shoulder. As I turned around slowly, I looked from head to toe and I realised who it was, the demon headmaster. I looked up at him, I slowly backed away and twisted the door handle. *Whoosh!* I made a run for it. He was coming after me. I tripped and fell...

Lillie Griffiths (12)
St Columbanus' College, Bangor

Ran Down

I couldn't run for much longer, my feet were numb with pins and needles crawling up my leg. My waist was killing me with stitch after stitch but I knew I had to keep going. I knew they were near. It was dark and foggy. I could hardly see where I was going. All I could see was the bright stream of light of a flashlight, chasing after me. Running for my life, I tripped over a log and fell rapidly to the ground. I saw the flashlight getting closer and closer. They were near. I hid. My heart stopped.

Ross David McBride (14)
St Columbanus' College, Bangor

On The Run

I could feel the ground shake beneath my trembling feet, this is how I knew it was getting closer. My heart pounded as though it was trying to jump out of my chest. What was this creature and what did it want from me? As the pulsing of the ground grew stronger, I saw a dark, strange figure getting closer. It wasn't like anything I had ever seen before. I got up off the slippery ground and ran! My legs burned. I couldn't run for much longer. My legs gave in and I fell, hitting the cold, hard ground.

Grace Veale (13)
St Columbanus' College, Bangor

I Escaped

11pm, our master plan was in action. We crawled out of the smashed window and ran without looking behind us. When the lights were not pointed at us and the cameras could not see us, we heard a shot and realised that one of us had been shot. My friend said, "We have to leave, now, or we will get caught." We ran and climbed over the wall as fast as we could until we found the woods. We looked behind us and we could see the police, we heard the sirens but we continued to run. We escaped.

Taylor Quayle (12)
St Columbanus' College, Bangor

A Psycho Who Tried To Kill Me

I couldn't run for much longer. I was on my phone when my kitchen door opened, I thought it was my brother and sister coming back from a friend's place but it was only 6:30pm and my parents were at work. I slowly got up to see who it was. It was someone else. He looked like he had escaped from prison. He saw me so I ran outside. He tried to shoot me and I barely managed to dodge them. That's when the police caught him. I don't know what would have happened to me if I was shot.

Jordan Kuruvilla (13)
St Columbanus' College, Bangor

Help Me

I still have nightmares about the day this old man started chasing me to kill me. I ran into my room, locked the door and all I heard was banging on the door. Then all of a sudden, the banging stopped. So, I unlocked my bedroom door and opened it. No one was there but I knew that he didn't go away, he was waiting for me somewhere, I just didn't know where. I knew this was a bad idea but I walked around my house to look for him. I looked everywhere but I couldn't find him. Help me!

Anastazia Bariova (12)
St Columbanus' College, Bangor

Hunted

I couldn't run for much longer. My legs burned so much. I was running that fast. Crying as I ran. I was so scared he would catch me. I felt sick to my stomach. My heart was racing... but I knew I couldn't stop, not even for a second. I could hear my mum screaming my name, she was a mess, I could hear it in her voice. She was crying and panicking, struggling to breathe. She was crying so much. I knew he was still chasing me, so I couldn't shout to my mum as he would hear me.

Amy Claney (13)
St Columbanus' College, Bangor

The Dangerous Crown

I couldn't run for much longer. I had to leave the country as fast as I could. I was accused of stealing the crown but I didn't steal it... someone framed me. I'd been running for hours. I thought I was lost, all alone in this world. I was almost at the border but when I got there, I was put in a van by these masked men. They locked me up, no one could hear me shouting for help. They asked me if I could give them the crown or else. I told them I didn't have the crown...

Olivia Maya Watson (12)
St Columbanus' College, Bangor

The Space Chase

We had just gone through the nebular catching up to our ship, Red Dwarf, that had been taken over by androids. We were hunting her down. We had just gone through an asteroid-belt containing sirens to lure us down to crash on the asteroids. Some of our crew on Starbug-1 fell for it but we made it through in the end. With a broken oxygen unit, it was only a matter of time before our oxygen ran out. Red Dwarf was in sight, we sped our way to light speed to get to our home. We made it.

Cameron Wallace (13)
St Columbanus' College, Bangor

Hunted

The sirens wailed, it almost seemed like everything was in slow motion. All we could do was run because they were chasing us. I was losing my breath, I couldn't run for much longer. I needed to stop before I dropped to the ground. Oh, no, they found me. I had to run. I got up and started sprinting, they spotted me and ran after me. When I lost them, I saw a man lying on the floor. I couldn't just leave him so I went over and helped him but before we started running. They got us...

Remi-Rose Brotherston (13)
St Columbanus' College, Bangor

Lost

"Goodnight," said my mother. That was the last time I heard her voice as I had been kidnapped from my home. I had been brought to a place that was very horrible, it was like a dungeon. I had been there for around two months and was building an escape plan to get out and back to my family. I was planning to cut a tile out of the room I was staying in, climb onto the roof and get out.

When I cut the tile off, I stuck my head out and smelled fresh air. Finally...

Dominik McCasland (13)
St Columbanus' College, Bangor

The Beast

Where can I hide now from this monster? It has been a while since I stopped... I don't even know how long I've been here, I'm all tired out. As I look for a place to hide, I hear a piercing howl. I stand there shaking from head to toe. I know that it is coming closer. I look from side to side if there is a spot to hide. I hear something falling down. I turn around and see a large, hairy figure standing high on a cliff, a ray of moonlight shining on the beast.

Nikola Kula (12)
St Columbanus' College, Bangor

Nightmare

I still have nightmares about the night I was almost kidnapped.

It was freezing outside and I was walking home from my friend's house when this horrifying looking man started chasing me. I began to run as fast as my little legs would take me but that was no good, he grabbed me by the collar and shouted at me to come with him. My heart started racing. Luckily, I got away. I sprinted home. I told my mum everything. She rang the police and he was never seen again.

Kiana McGimpsey (11)
St Columbanus' College, Bangor

The River

I couldn't run any longer, any time I took a breath it felt like needles hacking at my throat, down into my chest. I couldn't take it any longer. I had finally escaped the facility. I had followed a long, winding path that brought me to a river. I got in a boat and the water whirled around the base, taking the form of the rickety, old frame. I rowed down the stream and it became oddly quiet, it felt safe, oblivious of what was beneath me and what was to come.

Ruby Ward (13)
St Columbanus' College, Bangor

I Only Had 24 Hours To Escape

I only had twenty-four hours to escape Area 51. There were aliens everywhere I looked. I turned to my left and there was a massive alien right beside me. Thank god it didn't see me and I could try and make a run for it before it did. As I started running, I realised I only had ten minutes to get out alive. I heard them running behind me. They were fast, one grabbed at my arm with his big hand. He let go and I got out just in time but one got out and so I ran.

Jack Rendell (11)
St Columbanus' College, Bangor

Running

I couldn't run for much longer, the man I put in jail for murder was after me... ten years later, he was looking for revenge.

I was in a forest, I heard something beside me. I quickly lay down. I saw him, it looked like he was just at my house but he did not have on his mask for when he kills people. He stood there trying to find something, he started to dig into the ground. He dug out a mask and under the mask, there was an axe. He turned around...

Aaron Abraham (12)
St Columbanus' College, Bangor

Kidnapped

I had twenty-four hours. I got kidnapped one rainy day. I got into a stranger's car, he told me he was my neighbour and I believed him... I thought he was taking me home. We went to a little farmhouse. He grabbed my arm and dragged me into the basement. I begged him to let me go but he didn't listen, he told me I needed to escape and luckily I did. I found a key and it let me out. I found a weapon but I didn't use it on him, I used it to get out.

Adrianna Andrijauskaite (13)
St Columbanus' College, Bangor

On The Run

I couldn't run for much longer, my legs ached. I had been running for three miles. I was so thirsty. I had run out of food and water. I decided to stop and have a rest. I fell asleep for hours because it was dark. I knew there was a shopping centre close by so I decided to walk there. When I got to the shopping centre, it was closed. I needed to hide so I went to the shop behind it. I knew that they were still going to be out searching and looking for me.

Bethany McClements (13)
St Columbanus' College, Bangor

24 Hours

I couldn't run for much longer, my head was burning up. I only had twenty-four hours to get out of this city. I found a boulder thing, I lay up against it to give my legs a break. I started to sleep, suddenly I felt lots of pains over my body. It was acid rain, it was burning my skin. I had to find shelter. I ran for shelter, I found a cave, it was big and dark. I looked in my pocket and found a torch. Then a radioactive land shark jumped out at me.

Kavan McGrattan (12)
St Columbanus' College, Bangor

The Run In

I only had hours to prepare, they were coming. I had helped put him in there but he got out. An old man called Jim and his son had escaped the mental hospital. He was coming for us, he would kill anyone who got in his way. I was terrified, I hadn't heard from Mum in weeks until I was told to stop running by Jim on my mother's phone. He had her, so I told him to meet me at the carpark at the top of my road. I was so scared but I had to run.

Charlie McInerney (12)
St Columbanus' College, Bangor

Asylum

We have to leave now. Run. That asylum is crazy, blood everywhere, people getting chopped up into pieces. Weird dogs with cuts all around their bodies. It is some kind of symbol but I don't remember. They have these big machines with people screaming inside of them. It is so weird and they have these doctors that say they want to kill me, but I escaped the asylum. They have been chasing me since but I think I've lost them...

Oliver Elliott (12)
St Columbanus' College, Bangor

Found

It had to be here somewhere. It couldn't be much further. I heard a noise from the bushes. It was getting dark now, I had to get home. I heard it coming up behind me. I turned around. The rough pads on its feet scraped my jacket as I got knocked to the ground. It held me down. Its big, brown eyes stared into mine. Its big, floppy tail wagged left to right.

"Ollie! I found you! Let's get you home."

Stephanie Bell (13)
St Columbanus' College, Bangor

Kidnapped

My eyes were burning, my legs were numb and my arms were exhausted from trying to break out of the big black box. There were no lights and a big steel door. I was kidnapped and put into the back of a black van. There was tape over my mouth and my feet were taped together. I noticed that we were in a forest in an underground bunker. I was so scared. I heard feet coming, I hid and stayed quiet.

Reece Peck Bellorby
St Columbanus' College, Bangor

Beginning Or End?

Fires burning, ashes everywhere, people helplessly crying. My eyes filled with tears and this was the moment I knew I had to change.

Ten years have passed, people still haven't recovered. No one knew what happened. I thought, *there must be a way to solve this!* I rushed to the library. Whilst I was looking through the books, I saw two blue eyes. They were so blue, it was like the calming ocean.

Later that night, I heard a knock on the door. It was the same girl but covered in all black. She had a bomb in her hand...

Tayra Erturk (11)
St Mary's CE High School, Cheshunt

Branded For Carnage

He has been walking for hours. His feet are starting to bleed but he can't stop moving... he can't let them find him again. It wasn't supposed to be this serious. Her sister wasn't supposed to run into the knife. It was just a harmless prank, she wasn't supposed to die. Her screams were short, it was different from the last time. She started screaming for her sister as her voice began to fade into the void of death. As she cried out in agony, her sister walked in.
One last job. I hold no prisoners.

Ariarne Charles-West (11)
St Mary's CE High School, Cheshunt

The Reality Dream

It was that dream, that same dream I kept having that haunted my sleep every night. It always started with happiness but always ended in death.

It was the next morning and I saw something in the sky, it looked familiar and then I realised it was from my dream. My nightmare was becoming a reality! It crashed into a lake and it was gigantic! It opened up and I saw it. The creature, the creature who would lead this nightmare to an end, once and for all. Except, we would also have to end by nightmares as well.

Taylen Sanchez Salcedo (11)
St Mary's CE High School, Cheshunt

Escape

Tears welled up in my eyes. I was about to die. The pounding got louder and more frantic and there were screams from above. That would soon be me if I waited for even a second longer. Pushing away fear and rational thoughts, I ran. I didn't stop. Crashing through crowds, I could still hear the pounding. I had to escape. I had to leave. Sirens wailed and I knew I was done for but still, I pushed on. I turned a corner only to see... him. This was it. I heard the gunshot before I even saw the gun.

Leah Kaye (11)
St Ninian's High School, Kirkintilloch

XII/VII/257AD Italy, Rome

Dear Diary,
I have twenty-four hours left to live. As you know, I am proud of my previous victories in the colosseum but this time I won't survive. I have finally found my superior on the battlefield. Whilst waiting for death, I glance at the marble floor, gleaming coldly in the moonlight. The stars glint cruelly like polished daggers. I hold my helmet in my hands and think of my childhood. Each memory is as painful as an arrow through my heart. Dawn is breaking, I must go.
This is Marcus Caecilia, signing off for the last time.

Cerys Heath (11)
Welland Park Academy, Market Harborough

YOUNG WRITERS INFORMATION

We hope you have enjoyed reading this book – and that you will continue to in the coming years.

If you're a young writer who enjoys reading and creative writing, or the parent of an enthusiastic poet or story writer, do visit our website **www.youngwriters.co.uk**. Here you will find free competitions, workshops and games, as well as recommended reads, a poetry glossary and our blog. There's lots to keep budding writers motivated to write!

If you would like to order further copies of this book, or any of our other titles, then please give us a call or order via your online account.

Young Writers
Remus House
Coltsfoot Drive
Peterborough
PE2 9BF
(01733) 890066
info@youngwriters.co.uk